Baby Bear's Adoption

by Jennifer Keats Curtis   illustrated by Veronica V. Jones

This is a fictional account of a real-life program. Wildlife biologists in Michigan tag and track mama bears so that when they find an orphaned cub, they can place him or her with an adoptive family. Volunteers sometimes come along to help and hold the cubs while the wildlife biologists are working—just like the kids in this story!

In most cases, it is illegal, and certainly unsafe, to ever bother a bear. The Michigan biologists in this story are trained professionals and are present whenever their helpers touch a bear.

One chilly February morning, my sister Finley and I were in the yard putting the head onto our monster snowman. My dad came out holding two big, netted paddles underneath his arms. "Time for an adventure, Braden and Fin!" he shouted.

The paddles turned out to be snowshoes. Dad helped us fasten the shoes and then handed us ski poles. Finley grabbed my pole and used it to push me over. I rolled my eyes. Finley is always doing stuff like that.

Once I was on my feet, Dad showed us how to use the snowshoes to walk on top of the snow. We quickly figured out that it's easiest to let Dad go first and walk in his footprints.

Finley tried to kick snow at me but she fell down. I rolled my eyes. I told you, Finley is always doing stuff like that.

Then, right in front of us was a big hole surrounded by old, dead limbs and some skinny twigs.

"That, children, is a bear den," said Dad, "and I have a surprise for you."

My dad is a scientist—a wildlife biologist actually—and part of his job is to work with other biologists to help orphaned black bears.

A mother bear (sow) takes care of the babies. The dad (boar) doesn't help. It's sad, but sometimes a mother bear dies. If a cub is young, he won't survive without a mom. If that happens, my dad and his team can help find a sow with cubs to "adopt" him.

In the winter, adult bears hibernate. They are asleep but they can wake up quickly when bothered. Cubs are usually born in January. Their mom moves them so that they can snuggle up to her to stay warm and drink milk. That's called nursing.

If Dad finds a den with a sow and babies, he and his team put a bright orange collar on her. This collar has a signal that the scientists can use to track her. If they need the mom, they know exactly where to find her.

With his team nearby, Dad used his flashlight to look into the den. Finley and I could see the bear's eyes flash! Dad used a dart gun with medicine to knock her out. We waited until Dad and the other biologists were sure the bear wasn't going to wake up and then he carefully climbed into the den.

We couldn't really see what was going on until Dad crawled out again. He smiled at us and held out his hands.

There were two squirming black balls of fuzz. If you guessed that they were cubs, you were right! He quickly handed the babies to us and told us to keep them as warm as their mom did. I put my cub inside my fleecy coat. Finley wrapped her bear in her scarf.

Using ropes, Dad and his team pulled the mom bear out of the den so that they could put on the collar and make sure she was healthy. They checked for mange (a disease that can make her fur fall out). They weighed her and even took out a little tooth.

Inside her tooth are rings that tell her age.
They will send the tooth to a lab so that
another scientist can find out how old she is.

That whole time, we did our jobs keeping
those babies nestled close and cozy.

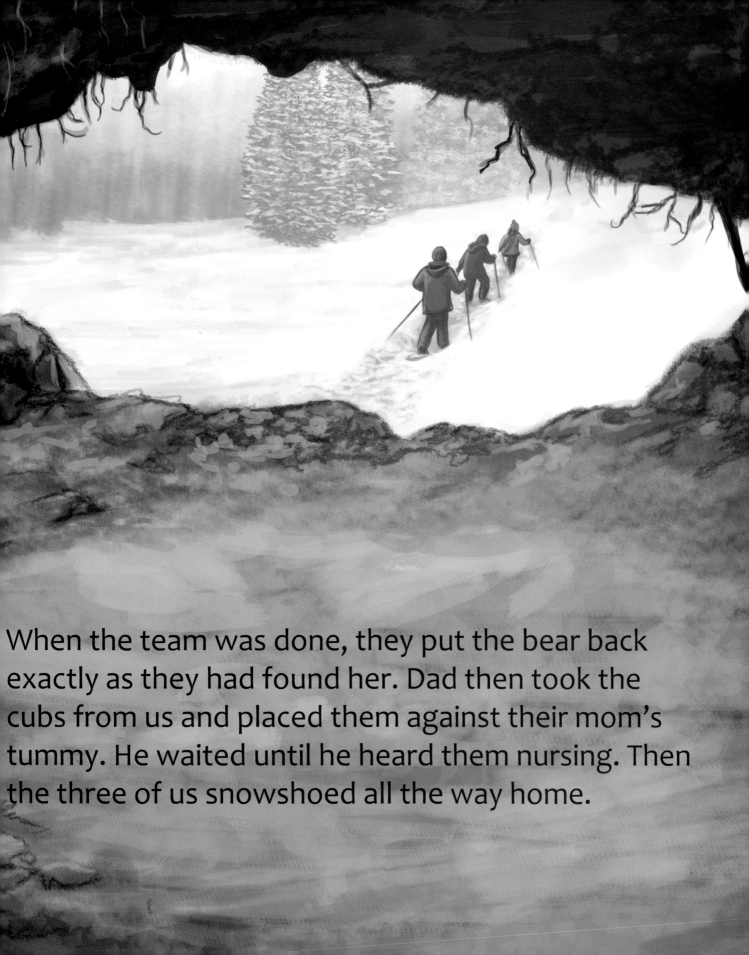

When the team was done, they put the bear back exactly as they had found her. Dad then took the cubs from us and placed them against their mom's tummy. He waited until he heard them nursing. Then the three of us snowshoed all the way home.

Finley and I thought about those bears
a lot. We drew pictures of them and
wondered if the mom would get to help an
orphaned baby that summer.

Then, in June, my dad got a call. A cub was sitting in a tree crying for his mom. He was making a distress call, which sounds like a little kid shrieking. Since the cub had been by himself overnight, Dad knew the bear's mom wasn't coming back.

This little guy needed help. Dad called a tree expert and they used a bucket truck to get the bear down. They put the baby into a box and took him to a safe place. Then they fed him special milk from a baby bottle.

To track the mom bear that we helped collar that winter, Dad and his team's pilot hopped into an airplane. They flew around until they picked up the signal from her collar.

Once they were back on the ground, Dad and his team gathered some equipment and the baby bear.

When Dad saw the sow and her cubs, he ran at her, waving his arms over his head and hollering. He wanted to scare her so she would tree the babies—tell them to run up a tree. Once the mom knew the cubs were safe, she would run away.

With the two cubs up a tree and the mom gone, they put stinky jelly all around the bottom of the tree where the cubs were. They took the baby they had rescued and covered him with the same smelly jelly. They placed him on the same tree where the other two babies were already sitting up high and watched him quickly climb to join his new brother and sister.

Dad and the other scientists backed away and hid behind a huge boulder. Then they waited.

After a while, the big sow came back calling for her babies. Her two cubs heard her and slid down the tree right through the goo.

The rescued baby followed.

When all three cubs were standing in front of her, the sow sniffed each of them. They all smelled the same. The rescued baby cooed right at her.

The mom bear grunted. She turned and started walking back into the woods. The whole family— her two cubs and the adopted baby—followed.

"Bears can't count?" asked Finley.

"I guess not," said Dad with a smile. I didn't even roll my eyes.

For Creative Minds

Black Bear Life Cycle

Put the black bear life cycle in order to discover the missing word.

The mama bear _____ the orphaned cub.

| O | By spring, the cubs weigh 10 pounds. They leave the den with their mom and learn how to forage for food. |

| T | By three years old, the bears are adults. They can find other adult bears and have babies of their own. |

| P | When the cubs are a year old, they are called yearlings. The yearlings stay with their mom until they are ready to leave and establish their own territory. |

| A | An adult female bear carries her cubs inside her for over 7 months. |

| S | Like all living things, bears eventually die. Most black bears in the wild live for 12-25 years. |

| D | The cubs are born in winter. Newborn cubs weigh about as much as a cup of yogurt. The cubs nurse and grow big in their winter den. |

Answer: The mama bear ADOPTS the orphaned cub.

Stages of Bear Hibernation

Hibernation

Hibernation can last up to seven months, depending on climate. Talk about a nice nap!

Walking Hibernation

A few weeks before the bear wakes up, its body temperature starts to rise. Metabolism returns to normal.

Scientists are still studying bears to figure out if bears are true hibernators or if they just go into a seasonal torpor. Hibernation is a very long nap; torpor is shorter. Hibernation is driven by the length of the day and hormones. Torpor has to do with temperature and food availability. During their winter sleep, black bears' body temperatures drop, their hearts beat more slowly, and they take fewer breaths than normal.

Metabolism is the process that changes food into energy for a living thing to use. Living things use energy in everything they do.

Normal Activity

During the spring and summer, bears eat and sleep. Black bears in some areas are active during the day (diurnal) and in other areas are active at night (nocturnal)

Hyperphagia

Bears need a lot of food to get ready for hibernation. They eat ten times more each day than a human, and drink gallons of water.

Animals store energy in their bodies as fat. Bears' bodies can use this energy during hibernation.

Fall Transition

Bears eat less as they get close to starting torpor. They won't pee or poop during their months in the den, so they don't want full bellies.

"hyper" = very
"phagia" = hungry

What do you think "hyperphagia" means?

Q&A with Bear Biologist Mark Boersen

Mark Boersen is a biologist with the Wildlife Division of the Michigan Department of Natural Resources (DNR). This book is based on the work Mark does with orphaned black bear cubs.

Did you know you wanted to be a scientist when you were a kid?

I always knew I wanted to be a scientist because I loved nature and learning how things work, but I didn't know what kind of scientist I wanted to be until 9th grade. My biology teacher had been a wildlife biologist. When he talked about his experiences and I learned I could get paid to study wildlife and their habitats, I realized that's it! I knew I wanted to be a wildlife biologist.

How and where do people usually find bear dens?

Sometimes people find bear dens when they are exploring outdoors. The DNR asks them to not disturb the animal, and to report the location to us. With smart phones and GPS, they can drop a pin and provide the exact location. Technology is really helpful!

Where are orphaned cubs found?

Orphaned cubs can be found anywhere in bears' normal range. A mother bear could become separated from her cubs at the den site, or a mother may be hit by a car when travelling in the spring. Cubs are most vulnerable from birth to six months old. There aren't many places that can take care of a bear this young, so we developed the collared bear program. We average one or two orphaned cubs in the program each year. Older cubs can find food and avoid danger on their own.

What's the trickiest part about working with bears?

Keeping track of where they are is tricky and requires a lot of time! Bears can cover a lot of ground. Some females stay within five miles of their dens, but bears can move up to 100 miles or more. We use aircraft and radio signals to help us track the collared bears.

What do you most enjoy about working with bears?

I love the hands-on work in the winter. I get to lead a team of wildlife professionals to bear den sites. The collaring program allows me to monitor the health of our bears, including newborn cubs. When I come back a year later to check on them, they've grown from little, helpless, five-pound furballs to 60-pound yearlings! Black bear sows are really good mothers. They put a lot of effort into caring for their young.

Furry Fun Facts

There are three types of bears in North America: black bears, grizzly bears (brown bears) and polar bears. Black bears are the smallest and the most common. They live in North America, from Canada and Alaska all the way down to Mexico and Florida.

	Black Bear	Grizzly Bear	Polar Bear
Scientific name	*Ursus americanus*	*Ursus arctos*	*Ursus maritimus*
height at shoulder	3 feet (0.914 meters)	4.5 feet (1.37 meters)	3.5-5 feet (1-1.5 meters)
average weight	180-200 lb. (82-91 kg.)	300-1200 lb. (136-544 kg.)	400-1200 lb. (181-544 kg.)
fur color	black, brown, cinnamon, blonde	brown with light tips	white
diet	mostly plants, some meat	both plants and animals	mostly meat, some plants

Like most bears, black bears eat both plants and animals (omnivores). They eat plants, fruits (they love berries), insects, honey, fish, small animals and animals that are already dead.

Bears will go dumpster diving and eat humans' trash. People who live in the same areas as bears lock their garbage cans so the bears won't get into them. Bears have such a keen sense of smell that they can sniff food in a car and break in to get it.

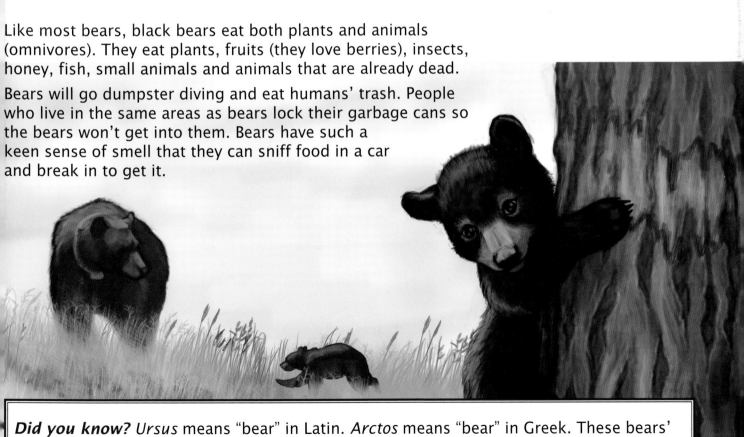

Did you know? *Ursus* means "bear" in Latin. *Arctos* means "bear" in Greek. These bears' scientific names tell us that the black bear is an American bear, the polar bear is a maritime (ocean) bear, and the grizzly is a bear-bear!

A big thank you to wildlife biologist Mark Boersen of the Michigan Department of Natural Resources (DNR) who generously shared his knowledge and photos during the research and writing of this book. Thanks also to Kevin Swanson and John Pepin, also of the Michigan DNR, for their assistance.—JKC

Thanks to Sara Focht, Wildlife Educator, Idaho Department of Fish and Game, for verifying the accuracy of the information in this book.

Library of Congress Cataloging-in-Publication Data

Names: Curtis, Jennifer Keats, author. | Jones, Veronica, illustrator.
Title: Baby bear's adoption / by Jennifer Keats Curtis ; illustrated by
   Veronica V. Jones.
Description: Mount Pleasant, SC : Arbordale Publishing, [2018] | Summary:
   Braden and Finley accompany their father, a wildlife biologist, when he
   tags a bear that has just had cubs and later, use the tag to find her
   again in hopes she will adopt an orphaned cub. Includes activities. |
   Includes bibliographical references.
Identifiers: LCCN 2018005025 (print) | LCCN 2018013249 (ebook) | ISBN
   9781607187523 (English Downloadable eBook) | ISBN 9781607187653 (English
   Interactive Dual-Language eBook) | ISBN 9781607187585 (Spanish
   Downloadable eBook) | ISBN 9781607187707 (Spanish Interactive
   Dual-Language eBook) | ISBN 9781607187264 (English hardcover) | ISBN
   9781607187400 (English pbk.) | ISBN 9781607187462 (Spanish pbk.) | ISBN
   9781607187523 (English eBook) | ISBN 9781607187585 (Spanish eBook)
Subjects: | CYAC: Wildlife conservation--Fiction. | Black bear--Fiction. |
   Bears--Fiction. | Orphaned animals--Fiction. | Animals--Infancy--Fiction.
   | Animal rescue--Fiction.
Classification: LCC PZ7.C941825 (ebook) | LCC PZ7.C941825 Bab 2018 (print) |
   DDC [E]--dc23
LC record available at https://lccn.loc.gov/2018005025

Lexile® Level: 640L Key phrases: environmental education, helping animals

Bibliography

"Black Bear Sounds." Bear Smart Durango. Bear Smart Durango, 2013. Web.
Boersen, Mark and Swanson, Kevin. Personal Interviews. 2017
Cox, Daniel J. *Black Bear*. San Francisco: Chronicle, 1990. Print.
Leeson, Tom, and Pat Leeson. *Black Bear*. Woodbridge, CT: Blackbirch, 2000. Print.
Swinburne, Stephen R. *Black Bear: North America's Bear*. Honesdale, PA: Boyds Mills, 2003. Print.

Printed in China, July 2018
This product conforms to CPSIA 2008
First Printing

Arbordale Publishing
Mt. Pleasant, SC 29464
www.ArbordalePublishing.com